Hello, Family Members,

Learning to read is one of the most important accomplishments of early childhood. **Hello Reader!** books are designed to help children become skilled readers who like to read. Beginning readers learn to read by remembering frequently used words like "the," "is," and "and"; by using phonics skills to decode new words; and by interpreting picture and text clues. These books provide both the stories children enjoy and the structure they need to read fluently and independently. Here are suggestions for helping your child *before*, *during*, and *after* reading:

Before

- Look at the cover and pictures and have your child predict what the story is about.
- Read the story to your child.
- Encourage your child to chime in with familiar words and phrases.
- Echo read with your child by reading a line first and having your child read it after you do.

During

- Have your child think about a word he or she does not recognize right away. Provide hints such as "Let's see if we know the sounds" and "Have we read other words like this one?"
- Encourage your child to use phonics skills to sound out new words.
- Provide the word for your child when more assistance is needed so that he or she does not struggle and the experience of reading with you is a positive one.
- Encourage your child to have fun by reading with a lot of expression . . . like an actor!

After

- Have your child keep lists of interesting and favorite words.
- Encourage your child to read the books over and over again. Have him or her read to brothers, sisters, grandparents, and even teddy bears. Repeated readings develop confidence in young readers.
- Talk about the stories. Ask and answer questions. Share ideas about the funniest and most interesting characters and events in the stories.

I do hope that you and your child enjoy this book.

— Francie Alexander
Reading Specialist,
Scholastic's Learning Ventures

For Fluffy fan Nelson Jaquan Lee, Jr.
— K.M.

For Gabrielle, who (almost) never misses the bus
— M.S.

Text copyright © 2000 by Kate McMullan.
Illustrations copyright © 2000 by Mavis Smith.
All rights reserved. Published by Scholastic Inc.
SCHOLASTIC, HELLO READER, CARTWHEEL BOOKS
and associated logos are trademarks and/or
registered trademarks of Scholastic Inc.

ISBN: 0-439-20671-5

Library of Congress Cataloging-in-Publication Data

McMullan, Kate.
    Fluffy's school bus adventure / by Kate McMullan ; illustrated by Mavis Smith.
        p.   cm. — (Hello reader! Level 3)
    "Cartwheel books."
    Summary: When Fluffy the guinea pig is accidentally put on the wrong school bus, he ends up having a wonderful time.
    ISBN 0-439-20671-5 (pbk.)
    [1. Guinea pigs — Fiction. 2. School buses — Fiction.]
I. Smith, Mavis, ill. II. Title. III. Series.
PZ7.M2295 Fg 2000
[E] — dc21   00-035782

10 9 8 7 6 5 4 3 2   01 02 03 04

Printed in the U.S.A.   24
First printing, October 2000

FLUFFY'S
SCHOOL BUS ADVENTURE

by Kate McMullan
Illustrated by Mavis Smith

Hello Reader! — Level 3

SCHOLASTIC INC.
New York Toronto London Auckland Sydney
Mexico City New Delhi Hong Kong

The Big Mistake

It was Friday afternoon.
"Good-bye!" Ms. Day called
to her students.

Ms. Day was about to go home, too.
But then she saw Fluffy.
"Fluffy!" said Ms. Day.
"Why are YOU still here?"

"Jasmine was supposed
to take you home," Ms. Day said.
"I guess she forgot."
Forgot? thought Fluffy.
**How could anybody
forget ME?**

"Maybe I can catch her,"
said Ms. Day.
She picked up Fluffy's cage and ran outside.
She hurried over to a school bus.
"Does Jasmine ride this bus?"
she asked the driver.
The driver nodded.

Ms. Day held up the cage.
"She forgot something."
That would be me,
thought Fluffy.

The driver took Fluffy's cage.
She put it on an empty seat.
"I will surprise Jasmine
when she gets off the bus," she said.
She started the bus and drove off.

A girl sat next to Fluffy.

She took him out of his cage.

"Have a lollipop, little pig," she said.

A what-a-pop? thought Fluffy.

He licked it.

The thing tasted yummy.

But it made his fur green and sticky.

"This is my stop,"
the girl said.
She gave Fluffy
to the boys behind her.
"'Bye, little pig."

The boys were playing
with purple goo.
"Have some goo, little pig,"
they said.
They showed Fluffy
how to squish the goo
through his paws.
It turned his paws purple.
Oooooh! thought Fluffy.
The goo felt like cold jelly.

The boys put the goo back into a jar.
They gave Fluffy to the girl
behind them.

"'Bye, little pig," they said.
Fluffy and the girl
were the last ones on the bus.

The girl put her sunglasses on Fluffy.
She put glitter on him.
"You look like a rock star!" she said.
That's me! thought Fluffy.

The girl held Fluffy up to the window.
Some kids in another bus saw him.
They waved.
Rock Star Fluffy waved to his fans.

The bus stopped again.
The girl took the sunglasses
off Fluffy.
She carried him
to the front of the school bus
and gave him to the driver.
"Wait," said the driver.
"Ms. Day asked me
to give the pig to you, Jasmine."

"I'm not in Ms. Day's class,"
said the girl.
"That's Jasmine P.
I'm Jasmine M."
And she got off the bus.

Fluffy looked at the bus driver.
The bus driver looked at Fluffy.
Uh-oh, they both thought.
There has been a BIG mistake!

Fluffy Helps Out

"I know where Jasmine P. lives,"
the bus driver told Fluffy.
"I will take you to her house."
She put Fluffy into her pocket.
She drove off.
Make way for the bus!
thought Fluffy.

The driver stopped at a red light.
All of a sudden,
the bus went *CA-LUNK!*
The engine stopped.
Uh-oh, thought Fluffy and
the driver.

The bus driver called a tow truck.
The tow truck driver put a big hook
on the bumper of the school bus.
The tow truck picked up
the front end of the bus.
Now THAT is strong,
thought Fluffy.

The bus driver and Fluffy got
into the tow truck.
Make way for the tow truck,
thought Fluffy.

They stopped at a garage.

"What is the trouble?" asked the mechanic.

"The engine went *CA-LUNK!* and stopped,"
the bus driver said.

The mechanic opened the hood.

He bent over the engine.

He opened caps.

He poked around.

He tried to start the bus.

Nothing happened.

"Are you sure it went *CA-LUNK?*"
he asked. "Or did it go *CLANK?*
Or maybe *CLINK?*"

"It went *CA-LUNK!*"
said the bus driver.
She bent way over the engine.
Fluffy fell out of her pocket.
Yowie! he cried.

Fluffy grabbed a rod.

It was oily.

He could not hold on.

He grabbed a cable.

It was greasy.

His paws slipped off.

He grabbed something that
looked like a rope.

Got it! thought Fluffy.

Fluffy held on to that rope.
He pulled himself up, up, up.
At last he poked his head
out of the greasy engine.
Here I am! thought Fluffy.

"The little pig found
a broken fan belt,"
said the mechanic.
"Now I can fix this bus."
The bus driver picked up Fluffy.
"Nice going, little pig!" she said.
It was dirty work, thought Fluffy.
**But somebody had
to do it!**

Fluffy's Pizza Party

The mechanic put in a
new fan belt.
By the time he finished,
it was suppertime.
"Let's order a pizza," he said.

"Good idea,"
said the tow truck driver.
"Yes," said the school bus driver.
"Let's have a pizza party
for the pig."
All right! thought Fluffy.
Party time!

The tow truck driver
phoned for the pizza.
The mechanic
turned on his radio.

Shimmy to the left, now, baby!
Boogie to the right!
Turn around, jump up and down!
Dance all night.

"Can you dance, little pig?"
the school bus driver asked Fluffy.
Who, me? thought Rock Star Fluffy.
He danced up a storm.

"The pizza is here!"
called the tow truck driver.
Everyone hurried
over to the table.
The pizza was topped
with red and green peppers.
Oh, boy! thought Fluffy.
He jumped on his slice
and dug in.

"Time to go, little pig,"
said the school bus driver.
Fluffy waved good-bye
to the tow truck driver
and the mechanic.

Then the bus driver put Fluffy
back into her pocket.
She got into the school bus.
It started right up.

On the ride to Jasmine's house,
Fluffy thought about his lollipop.
He thought about the purple goo
and about being a rock star.
He remembered riding in the tow truck
and how he helped fix the school bus.
He licked some pizza sauce
off his back leg.
What a day! thought Fluffy.
It doesn't get any better than this.

The bus driver rang Jasmine's bell.

"FLUFFY!" Jasmine cried

when she opened the door.

"You poor pig!"

"Oh, he's all right,"

said the school bus driver.

She winked at Fluffy.

"Good-bye, little pig!"

Jasmine took Fluffy inside.
"I'm sorry I forgot you,"
she said. "I will give you
a warm bath. I will feed you
carrots and apples.
I will tuck you into my doll bed
and rock you all night long."
She hugged Fluffy.
"Poor lost pig," she said.
"It must have been awful."

Yeah, thought Fluffy as he
snuggled under a warm blanket.
Just awful!